Bored By the Billionaire

A City Entanglements Novella

Tara Kennedy

Copyright

Table of Contents

Bored By the Billionaire (City Entanglements, #2) 1
Chapter 1...2
Chapter 2...7
Chapter 3.. 12
Chapter 4.. 17
Chapter 5.. 18
Chapter 6.. 21
Chapter 7.. 25
Chapter 8.. 28
Chapter 9.. 33
Chapter 10 39
Chapter 11 41
Chapter 12 46
Chapter 13 48
Chapter 14 52
Chapter 15 56
Chapter 16 60
Chapter 17 63
Chapter 18 68
Acknowledgements and Thanks.. 71
Next in the series: 72
About the Author.. 73
Also By Tara Kennedy 74
Clear as Ice 75

To my family, near and far. The storytelling genes are all from you all. Stories are how we connect and support. This year has definitely shown that.

Chapter 1

Lucinda "Lulu" Wei Williams looked around the party. She was wearing a fabulous dress, sipping expensive champagne, and surrounded by a combination of rich and swank people. And she was bored.

"Lucinda, don't you agree, Koi was just not quite worth the hype. Charming but," Richard tipped his head as if searching for the right term. He had given this spiel five times tonight, and she could practically recite it along with him now. "Not special. I wish them well of course. So hard to start a new restaurant these days," he said.

When word had first spread of the new modern Asian fusion place with a chef's table like set up, and only 50 seats per night, Richard had offered to invest. He hoped to look hip and on trend, and also, to be the guy who could tell all his friends that he could get them a table. But the owners had said they were keeping investors to a minimum. They had still gotten a table opening week, but now Richard was sure it was a passing fad.

Richard slid his arm around her waist and pressed a kiss to her ear. Instead of thrilling and exciting Lulu, it just added to her ennui. Billionaires were great when they first decided they wanted you. Jetting off on exclusive first dates to places it was often hard for someone not third generation this, that, or the other to get into without connections. But Lulu found after a month or two, they thought a fundraising dinner like this one, counted as a date. The cause was worthy, but the cost of the dinner and the champagne meant they needed donations on top of the thousand dollar a head entry fee to actually have enough left over for the charity. And the company tonight had not made it more interesting.

Lulu liked wearing pretty dresses, she liked drinking expensive drinks, and she liked going home and having sex after.

But while Richard looked great in his tux tonight she had to admit, if he fell asleep in the limo ride back to his place, she'd be okay.

So, here she was — bored by the billionaire. They said their goodbyes to the couple who were moving to the next group. She turned to Richard. "Hey, sweetie," she said keeping her voice low. Rich people were the worst gossips in her opinion.

"Yes, my dear?" Richard said.

"I'm going to head home tonight. I think we're at a natural endpoint. No hard feelings, okay." She smiled and kissed his nose, while moving away from his arm and waved prettily behind her as she exited the ballroom. She went down a hallway, where she had seen an exit sign before, made her way up the fire stairs to the lobby, and peeked around carefully. Richard wasn't abusive or even particularly hot-tempered. But he would want to talk about this, long enough to convince himself that this breakup was his idea. Lulu could care less whose idea he told people it was, she just didn't want to spend three hours helping him process the breakup. Quick, clear, easy was her style. She spotted a hotel employee.

"Hey, I'm not in danger, but if I wanted to get outside without running into anyone in the lobby, what's my best route?"

The woman gave her an assessing look. "Do you need to find a limo or taxi?"

Yeah. Lulu probably should have waited to break up with Richard until they were waiting for the car. But he normally wanted to stay til the bitter end, hobnobbing with the same people he'd seen at last week's soiree, and she just needed out.

"That would help, but I'm going to rideshare, so I can find my way once I'm on the street." Or let the GPS do it. She knew her way around New York these days. But she had a condo in DC with a couch that was desperately calling out to her. Richard had called her condo quaint. She hadn't bothered to tell him about how the value had already increased from when she bought it. Or that stabilizing her mortgage had been on her bucket list after growing up where they moved all across the suburbs trying to outrun rising housing costs.

Of course lately between consulting with the factory reps out in California, and dating Richard, she had barely seen her couch. Which was the other reason she hadn't bothered to upgrade her housing. She had bought a house for her parents out in the suburbs, teaming up with her brother to convince them to let them do this. Lulu's brother worked as a teacher, so basically he had bought the curtains, and Lulu had bought the rest. She'd buy her brother a place if he'd let her, but so far he refused to move, having found a decent rent controlled place in DC.

Lulu's hotel savior Jessica led her through an employee only entrance, waving at other employees who clearly were curious about Lulu, nodded and let them pass. Reaching a door marked with signs about not allowing re-entrance, Jessica popped it open to reveal a sidewalk. "If you need the subway, you can go three blocks that way. You sure you're okay?"

"I'm grand. Thanks so much for helping me. Breakups are just a little awkward at first." Lulu smiled.

"Great purse, by the way," Jessica said.

"Thanks. Oh," she popped open her small clutch, one of her own creations, and pulled out a card. "Email me, I know the owner, I can get you one as a thank you."

"Oh, you don't have too," Jessica said shaking her head.

"I know I don't. I want to. Please take the card."

Jessica took the card and tucked it into her pocket. Lulu smiled and waved and then headed down the street a bit, to blend in better with anyone else in fancy dress wandering around. Not hard in this part of New York. The GPS on her phone told her the train station was farther than these fancy heels were going to get her. She stopped, slip them off, pulled out the fold up in her purse, and slid them on, wiggling her toes in relief. Not quite as good a match to the dress as the heels, but her feet weren't screaming, and she thought the flats were cute, if not quite black tie.

The rideshare app said ten minutes which was the problem with hanging on the rich people side of town. So, she'd walk to the subway. The heels didn't fit in her purse, so she carried them.

Another reason to stop dating billionaires. It was so much easier to exit quickly when not in fancy dress.

LULU GOT A COUPLE OF glances on the subway, but the nice thing about late night public transit was that you were hardly ever the oddest thing. She broke out the credit card at Penn Station. Last minute sleeper cars were priced ridiculously, and she was again grateful to have left Richard behind, at that party, in her life, in everything. He would have insisted on the sleeper car, instead of the perfectly fine for one evening regular seat.

Sure, her little purse business as another ex had once referred to it was doing well, and she and her partner were finalizing a much teased shoe expansion. But just because her bank account now held more than she'd ever dreamed didn't mean she didn't remember the lean years growing up. Or the lean years when she and her business partner Maya lived on ramen, and rice topped with ketchup packets they'd stolen from fast food places while they waited for their first products, their first orders.

Richard couldn't imagine a day when his bank account wouldn't have the same number of zeroes. Lulu didn't think every choice in her life had to be the most expensive one.

Once they began boarding, the group moved down the tracks. Looking around at her fellow travelers, it was a mix of folks in business clothes, or folks who looked in vacation mode, with flip-flops and baseball caps. No one else was in fancy dress, and part of her wished she had picked up a blanket scarf from one of the vendors in the station.

She followed directions to the quiet car and sat down, sliding to the window seat, tucking her clutch next to her.

She hadn't thought to put her earbuds in the clutch which was a mistake she would make a note not to make again. Hopefully the ambient noise of the train would be sufficient. Now that she was sitting and had nothing to do for the next few hours, all the energy that had gotten her out of the hotel and here, seemed to have dribbled out of her.

A dude paused next to her, "This seat open?"

Lulu sighed, but nodded. She glanced around, the train was pretty full, although she was still sure there were seats elsewhere. This man in his admittedly well-made work suit better not think anything was happening other than them sharing the same train for a few hours.

He slid his leather messenger bag under the seat and sat down, situating himself without managing to encroach past the armrest or to manspread. His cologne was subtle and spicy, just enough that she almost wanted to lean in and get a better sniff.

But, Lulu reminded herself, she had been single for about an hour. She certainly didn't need to take up with a dude who was still wearing a suit, even a well-made one, at this hour of the night.

Chapter 2

Aiden Camden George tried to glance subtly at the woman seated next to him. The orange dress looked stunning on her seated in a train car. He was pretty sure if he had the chance to see her standing he might have his first and last heart attack.

His friend's play had opened off Broadway tonight. Aiden had stayed long enough to congratulate him but, the hotel business never stopped. So here he was on a train back to DC. But hey, he was seated with an attractive woman and maybe he would get more than sleep on this train ride.

Her dress looked a little fancy for theater, although you never knew what people in the box seats were going to wear.

"I saw a great show tonight," he said.

She smiled politely.

"Were you at the theater?" he asked. The train began moving and there were various announcements about tickets, stations and such.

She looked back at him, and her eyes were amazing. Aiden liked the female form, but often found he didn't really get attracted to folks until he knew a little more about them. For all he knew she had been in New York buying snakes for her snake handling act. He had a live and let live policy for snakes, as in they could live anywhere not near him.

"No," she answered finally. "Boring party."

"That's unfortunate," he said. He had been to a number of events that went by the name party but were anything but. "They shouldn't be allowed to call themselves that."

"I'm sorry?" she said.

"Oh, I just meant, if it's boring, it's not really a party. Party implies fun. The events that are not fun, should not get to call themselves parties. There should be another word."

She giggled and the sound poked inside him, like the slide of caramel or honey down his throat. He shifted in his seat only to find the conductor standing over them.

"Tickets?" he asked.

They handed over their phones. "Two DCs." The conductor handed back their phones and placed the punch cards above them. "Remember, this is the quiet car. Only quiet talking."

Aiden nodded. He had not planned on doing more than resting on this train trip. But he could flirt quietly.

"What would we call them?" she asked softly. "No one would go to something called a snoozy."

"Pancakes."

"Pancakes?" she leaned closer, like she was trying to make sure she heard correctly.

He kept his voice low, hoping she would lean even closer. "It's perfect. Everyone gets very excited about pancakes, but in reality, pancakes are flat and boring, and people only really like the things they stick on top of them."

"I feel like there's some deep-seated pancake harm was done to you in childhood. What about blueberry pancakes, or chocolate chip pancakes?"

"Wouldn't it be better to just have blueberries or chocolate chips?" Aiden asked.

"Fair point. Okay. Change approved." She held out her hand and he grasped it. Her skin was soft as he had imagined. He felt ridiculously pleased, like he had passed a test, gotten excellent customer feedback, and downed a shot of tequila all at the same time. Was it possible the celebratory shots backstage had only now kicked in?

She shifted again and kicked off her sandals. He noticed the fancier heels tucked next to them.

She smiled, "Sorry, my feet are just." She shrugged not finishing the sentence.

"May I help?" He held his hands out, belatedly realizing it was probably not done to offer to massage a stranger's feet. But he had held jobs where he stood a lot, and had learned a few things about soothing tired feet, although he usually didn't have to wear heels. "Sorry if that seems creepy. I just, well, I'd like to help."

"Are you a foot fetishist?" she asked but her tone sounded more curious than suspicious, and she shifted again, placing one of her feet near his lap.

He adjusted so he could cradle it in his hands, realizing as he did so, what a weird and strange night this was turning into. He stroked lightly along the sole of her foot, and then used thumbs to press against some of the pressure points. She moaned and he looked over. "Okay?" he asked.

"Perfect," she said, and the sound made his whole body tighten.

He pressed again and she moaned and he was unable to ignore how much he wanted to see if she moaned like that during sex. This was a weird and strange night where he had ended up giving a foot massage that was turning into his most erotic experience this year.

He pressed into her foot with his thumb again, and she moaned. Her eyes were closed but she slowly opened them. The expression in her face warned him, right as she shifted pulling her foot out of his lap. The conductor was in the aisle next to him, Aiden hadn't even heard him approach.

"You two have been warned. Come on, we're going to need you out of the quiet car."

Aiden was about to protest, about to promise they'd be quieter. But the looks on the passengers across the aisle, and peeking into it from other rows, told him that enough customers wanted them gone. Aiden willed his body to forgive him for trying to stand and move about in this condition. Aiden was a little embarrassed, as someone who made customer service his career, to have become the problem customer. He grabbed his messenger bag, offered to hold one of the pairs of shoes for the lady, but she declined. They followed the conductor to another car.

"There aren't many seats together left, but we're stopping in Newark soon, so you might be able to find something." With that the conductor headed back the other direction.

Aiden wished he knew the punch card codes, so he could figure out who was disembarking soon. He turned back to her and decided maybe chatting with her until they reached the station would convince her to stick with him. "I'm Aiden, by the way. I don't usually cause commotions," he held out his hand.

"But, puns and rhymes are normal? Pancake hatred? Oh, I'm Lulu," she shook his hand.

He wanted to kiss her, but even though he'd touched her feet, something he wasn't sure he'd ever intentionally done with his last lover, it seemed too forward. She smelled like citrus and he wanted to learn what her mouth tasted like. He let go of her hand before he embarrassed himself. "Lulu," he repeated. "Wait, did I rhyme?"

"Oh, right," she laughed, "I guess that was my brain that rhymed. You said commotion, and I rhymed it with locomotion, because, you know, train."

He smiled as the ridiculous idea that he might already love her brain occurred to him. "You're right, commotion is, well, it's not usually the word I would have used. So that would explain why it came into my head before trouble, or all the obvious ones."

"Or, you're tired, and instead of sleeping, you were kind enough to try and massage my feet and I got us kicked out of the quiet car," Lulu said.

"Wait, I started us talking, I decided to massage your feet, I'm the one who got us the first warning, it's at least half my fault."

She shrugged. "Fine, it's half your fault for being good at massaging feet. Is feet massage your trade?"

"No, I work in a hotel."

"Does your hotel offer foot massages?" Lulu asked.

"It doesn't, although we have a deal with a nearby spa, for folks who inquire."

She touched his shoulder and pointed. A couple on the other end of the car was gathering up their things. They headed down slowly, allowing the couple to reach the door before they took their seats. She slid in first, and he followed.

"I should let you get some sleep," he said. He had gotten her name. He was confident he could get her number before they disembarked in DC, so that was enough for now.

She leaned in closer. "Or maybe now I should offer to massage you."

Chapter 3

Lulu should be embarrassed that she had moaned so much she'd been kicked out of the quiet car for sex noises. The sensible Lucinda side reminded her she had now been single for about ninety minutes, she should not be contemplating the next notch in her bedpost just yet. But the bold Lulu, who had grand ideas that she jumped into and figured out how to execute later — well, Lulu wanted to know if a man who knew his way around her feet, knew his way around the rest of her body.

This man, this Aiden, he wasn't another stuffy billionaire. Besides, if there was an appropriate timeframe for a rebound bang, wasn't it after the breakup, but before you had fully processed the end of it? One didn't become a member of the thirty under thirty lists, without taking advantage of the opportunities that the universe provided you. Would the universe have sent her a handsome man only to massage her feet and not the rest of her? Lulu had more faith in the universe than that. And while she didn't think sex on a train was the best way to explore that, she could at least let Aiden know that sleep had slipped lower on her immediate needs list.

"I really do not want to find out what happens if I start making sex noises on this train," he said.

She pouted her lips in sadness, even if it was a valid point. "You are heading to DC?" she asked, although she knew that.

"Yes, and you are too," he said. "I have a thing at ten, but before then," he trailed off.

The train was scheduled to arrive in DC around three am. That would give them at least six hours. It seemed like so much, and not nearly enough.

She leaned forward and kissed him. His mouth opened and their tongues met and holy crap, this was better than the foot massage.

She shifted closer, running a hand across his chest, wishing she could get underneath, to his skin.

The train lurched and bounced. He held her tight, his arms and hands grasping her butt to keep her from falling to the floor.

She pulled back from his lips, gratified to see the same stunned expression in his eyes. Lulu moved back into her seat, worried that if she tasted any more of him, she wouldn't be able to stop. He was addictive. They were addictive together.

"So," she said shifting her dress so it wasn't hiked up quite so high on her hip, "you said you worked in a hotel?"

"Yes," he said carefully.

She wondered if he was embarrassed to tell her that he was a room service attendant, a cleaner. She didn't care either way.

"Does that mean you have access to rooms there?" Lulu asked. "I can pay, I just, if you have to be there at ten, is it faster if we are already there?"

"Yes, and don't worry, I get a discount." He pulled out his phone and took a shaky breath. He tapped on his phone. "They'll have a key waiting."

"And you're sure you don't want me to pay?" she asked, looking closely, trying to make sure he wasn't endangering his rent or, god forbid, his kids or anything for sex. Lulu was confident in her skills, but no one needed to endanger their bank account over this. She could afford this, would happily stuff down her frugality to get this man inside her.

"I'm sure," he said. He kissed her nose. "We probably should try to sleep now, so that," he trailed off.

She shifted, putting her head on his shoulder, "So that I can exhaust you later?"

"Exactly so," he said.

LULU HELD AIDEN'S HANDS and tried to stay hard in Lulu land. She had drifted off to sleep only to lurch awake as the train pulled into Union Station in DC. The air felt cold, as they walked swiftly toward the hotel. The hotel was cute, in that modern chic way that suggested it was moderately priced. Well, moderate for downtown DC, which was a different scale than the hotels that dotted the suburbs, or further out.

They moved inside. An employee handed Aiden an envelope and Aiden thanked him. They were in the elevator before she wondered if she should offer to pay again. As the elevator door closed, he kissed her, fast and hard. The elevator door opened and he tugged her down the hallway. Lulu patted her hip, making sure her clothes hadn't already combusted, she still had her purse, her shoes.

Aiden paused and slid the key card into a door slot,. He scanned the room carefully as they entered. The room had a large bed, and a small writing desk over by the window. The door swung shut, Aiden's arms wrapped around her waist and he kissed her again, his whole body pressed against the length of hers.

She slid her hand under his suit jacket, tugging at the shirt, but she couldn't get to skin, she wanted his skin. She pulled away from his lips opening her eyes, reaching for buttons, but her hands kept fumbling them, and she let out a growl of frustration.

Aiden put his hands over hers, "Let me." He removed he jacket, his shoes, his pants, and started working on the shirt as she watched.

A sudden thought struck her. "Tell me you have condoms." She hadn't brought any in her purse. And if she had to get in a cab to go to her apartment or a twenty-four hour drug store she would, but all of that would take time.

He paused, his shirt unbuttoned over his black boxer briefs. He should look ridiculous, but Lulu kept thinking more of this please. He crossed to the bathroom, picked up a small shaving kit, and produced a sleeve of condoms.

"Oh good," she said.

He kissed her quickly going back to finish undoing the buttons. He got the shirt and the socks removed. She looked at the planes of his chest, smooth enough that she wondered if he shaved it or was naturally smooth. His skin was light olive, darker at his hands and feet, suggesting someone who didn't see much sun, and didn't bother to self tan. And his cock strained against those boxer briefs. She reached out a hand and stroked it the way she had wanted to on the train. She learned how it felt in her hand, listened to his breath catch as she stroked a little deeper.

His voice tickled along her ear, "Do you need help getting out of that dress?"

She didn't. She didn't believe in clothes one needed an assistant to maneuver, but she turned and let him undo the zipper. He pressed kisses along her shoulder and her back, as he slowly worked the zipper down. She slid her arms out, once he got the zipper to the bottom the dress slid and pooled at her feet. He flicked open her bra, and she slid that off too, feeling the cool hotel air over her body, her nipples tightening further. He pressed against her back, sliding his hands around to cup her breasts. Looking to the side, she realized there was a full length mirror. He watched her, as he stroked his thumbs across her nipples, pressing his lips to her neck.

One of his hands moved lover, cupping her through her panties, teasing her slit through the silky fabric. He moved his fingers inside, pressing against her clit, stroking one long finger inside her. She tightened around him, as he pressed his thumb against her clit, and pinched the nipple in her other hand. She moaned.

"Can you come like this?" he whispered against her ear.

She nodded, not wanted to distract with words. He stroked, and pinched, and then added a second finger inside her curling it back. He stroked harder against her clit, and she shuddered and came, huffing and moaning as she did. He kept hold of her as she finished, then gently slid out of her, turning her around to press a kiss to her lips. He licked his fingers.

She shimmied out of the panties, that now felt tight, damp, restrictive. She grasped the waistband of his boxer briefs, slowly peeling them down to reveal his very hard cock.

"Bed," he said and she nodded. They climbed on top of the comforter, and he paused to put the condom on. She lay on her back, legs open, and he moved over top of her. He pressed a kiss to her lips, "Ready?" he asked.

She didn't have words for how ready she was, how much she wanted him inside of her, so again she nodded. He pushed inside her, and they both paused, feeling the way their bodies fit together. She shifted her legs around his waist, and they both groaned. He began to shift, to pump and she moved her hips, their bodies shifting apart and together, pushing him in an out. The tension, the friction, the slip of their bodies together built, their speed increased and she felt her orgasm start just as he shuddered against her. They lay there still for a moment, recovering.

He grasped the condom and pulled out. She sat up, suddenly not tired at all.

"What time is it?" she asked as he returned from the bathroom.

"Three thirty," he said.

"Good. Plenty of time left," she said with a smile.

Chapter 4

Aiden wished he could call in sick. He couldn't of course. One couldn't set up a liaison at the place where one worked, and call in sick and expect anyone to take it seriously.

But right now, he was about to reach a personal best for orgasms in a single night. He was probably going to need eight to twenty-four hours to recover.

Lulu returned from the bathroom. "Do you need to nap a little?"

The responsible answer was yes. She had slept on the train. He had been unable to stop staring at her sleeping, watching her chest rise and fall, feeling her pressed against one side of his body. Every time he closed his eyes, he was worried she would wake up, and move away, she would come to her senses and realize he was a stranger.

He moved back to the bed and she followed, lying on her side to face him.

"I didn't even ask if you needed sleep," he said.

"I'm fine," she said.

After another round of orgasms, they pulled apart. He got up to toss the condom. Her eyes were closed when he returned. He managed to pull the blanket over both of them. He wondered if she was still awake or just pliant enough to let him curl around her before he fell asleep himself.

Chapter 5

The buzzing woke them both. Lulu sprang awake confused about who, what, where, and why.

It came back to her as Aiden's groggy voice said, "Sorry, that's for me." He slid off the bed and moved towards his pants. She got an excellent view of his ass as he leaned down to grab the phone and silence the noise. She couldn't help smiling at him. He smiled back. "I need to go, but before I do," he took in a breath, and she held hers, ready for whichever direction his next words would take them. Six, or was it seven orgasms, hadn't softened her. She would be fine with our without this man's excellent ass in her life. "You can stay here for a bit, I can handle things with the room. But either way, I'd love to see you again, in or out of a hotel room."

Lulu sat up. Terms, she was good at negotiating terms, even if they had failed to do so before now. "I just got out of a relationship. I assume you are single?"

He nodded. "Of course."

She wondered if it was naivete that had him saying of course, there was no of course about that. But, perhaps he meant of course, he only arranged hookups with strangers on trains when he was single. Perhaps that was true for him. It had sadly not been true for everyone she hooked up with.

"I'm not looking for serious," she said. "Just fun."

"I like fun," he said. "I would like to have fun, say tomorrow? I am off Sunday and Monday."

Lulu pictured her schedule in her head. She was supposed to have stayed in New York this weekend, relaxing, and working on the train back down Monday. She'd let her business partner Maya know she was here, rather than New York. She could afford to be a little flexible with her schedule especially if it would bring her well shaped butts. A well shaped butt in particular.

"I can be available," Lulu said. "Shall we meet for brunch Sunday?"

"Brunch is good."

"I'll text you where," she said.

He nodded. She sat there and watched him as he got ready. There was something sort of fascinating about watching him put himself together. The full length mirror by the door meant she could see him from where she sat on the bed even in the bathroom. Watch him brush his teeth, fix his hair, and straighten his shirt. She wondered if he wore the suit to work, or if he changed into some sort of hotel livery. There were certainly back office jobs where likely suits were normal. Maybe he was a shift manager. She would think about asking at brunch. Of course if she asked about his job, he would ask about hers. If he turned out to be a snob who snickered about there being money in making silly purses, she would have to cut him off, well shaped butt or no. So maybe she would wait before she asked.

When he came back out of the bathroom his eyes darkened looking at her, still naked and only partially covered by the sheet. She smiled, struck by an urge to mess up his hair.

"I want to kiss you, but I'm afraid I won't leave if I do," he said.

Her smile deepened as she imagined things she could do to him while he wore all those clothes, and even better all the things he could do to her.

"Yeah, that dangerous smile does not convince me. You'll text me about brunch?"

"Yes." Lulu waited until he had the door open before she said quietly, "Coward."

He glanced back at her with a smile of his own, that seemed full of promises, and then he left, the door swinging shut behind him.

Lulu felt hot and itchy, in attempting to rev him up a little, she had entirely succeeded in revving herself up.

She supposed waiting was good for the soul or something.

Lulu got home, checked in with her family, her business partner. Selected a brunch place, and texted Aiden. The DC area was littered with brunch places. Controlling the selection had partly been a test. If Aiden insisted he knew a better one, or that he should get to select, then, she had a good vibrator. Plus a phone that provided access to other eligible men. Sure, plenty of them would need a little guidance, a little instruction. The advantage of having given up billionaires again, was that many men were open to learning shortcuts to orgasms, since more orgasms, meant more sex. Also less standing somewhere while they made boring phone calls, and less fundraisers. Her job required plenty of fancy events on its own.

She put the phone to the side, determine not to stare at it waiting. Perhaps a nap was in order. She was hoping to get quite a workout Sunday.

Chapter 6

Today Aiden was especially grateful his parents worked out of the corporate offices in Silver Spring. On this conference call, they couldn't see all the silent communication happening in this room. But yes, he had known when he made a last minute reservation, that there would be talk. His staff were far too well-mannered to actually reveal any customer secrets, never mind that he wasn't a customer, but the manager. Having worked his way up from front desk attendant, meant he'd known everyone in this conference room a while.

So today there were sly smiles in the conference room, as they wrapped up the quarterly reports with his mother, who oversaw the financials for the entire chain.

"Everything sounds great, Aiden and team," his mother said. "I'll talk to everyone later. Thanks."

The phone signaled the conference call had ended, and Aiden sat back in his chair in the conference room.

Marcus raised his eyebrows at Aiden. "So, do we need to review the emergency bookings policy or are we clear on that?"

"I'm clear, thanks." Aiden said.

"The emergency booking Aiden made followed policy," Rhian said loyally, "he's just lucky we had a room available for him."

"Yes, I am," he said.

"And given that your guest has left, is it cleared to be cleaned, or do we need to hold it for another night?" Rhian asked.

"Clear to be cleaned. I let Shania know earlier." Aiden said. Rhian did not typically oversee specific room cleaning charts, since that was Shania's domain. So despite the loyal tone, Rhian was needling him. And, he admitted, it was fair. If Marcus had pulled this, he would have done the same. Heck, he may very well have insisted on sending up complimentary champagne to the room, because nothing like trying to maintain a mood when you knew you're entire team knew what you were up to.

As they moved out of the conference room, Marcus followed Aiden back to his office. Shutting the door, Marcus asked, "So, I thought you were going to New York to see a play. If I had known you were headed there to satisfy a sexual feeling," Marcus sang those words, "I might have joined you."

Aiden patted Marcus's shoulder. "Thanks, but you're not my type."

Marcus applauded. "Nice one. My girlfriend will be glad to hear that. But for real. Who is this lady who rates emergency bookings?"

"Still working on finding that out. I'll let you know." Aiden knew it was good that she had left. Just talking about her made him want to run back up to the room. So, it was a good thing she wasn't there, because he had several hours of work left. But brunch was another story.

AIDEN WAS RIDICULOUSLY pleased to see Lulu already seated when he arrived at the restaurant she had selected for brunch. The place had larger four, six, and eight tops throughout the main area of the floor. Lulu sat in one of the smaller booths, The booths were on raised platform around the three sides of the restaurant. Gauzy curtains provided a tiny bit of extra cover between each booth,without dangling too low to be a hazard for either patrons or staff. Lulu's booth was surrounded by two empty booths, the restaurant looked to be filling up, but not quite at peak capacity yet. As such the staff were being quick, but not hurried.

He slid into the booth. The semicircle shape allowed them to sit next to each other, hips, and thighs touching. His body tightened, already conditioned to hope nearness to Lulu would lead delightful places. "May I kiss you?" he asked leaning closer.

"Please," she whispered before placing her lips on his. Their mouths opened and tongues tangled. His hands, reached, and found her dress left her back bare, so he could touch skin, and his hands slid to the lowest boundary of that, teasing her waistband. Her hands tugged his polo shirt out of his pants, so she could touch the skin of his back. He wasn't sure how he was going to make it through brunch. They pulled apart, and he saw from her breathing, her pupils, she was just as affected as he was.

A waiter came up and poured them each a glass of water, leaving them a larger bottle for refills. Aiden considered dumping the whole thing on himself, or eyeing the frilly white halter thing Lulu had on, perhaps both of them.

They pulled open their menus. He tried to read the words. Aiden swore he used to know what waffles were, what was in eggs Benedict. He could feel her shifting next to him. She rubbed fingers over her collarbone, and he shifted in his seat. He used to have control. He used to be able to have food with people, even those he was sexually attracted to, and look forward to possibly having sex with them later. She shifted again, and he smelled that citrus scent.

The waiter returned and took their orders. Aiden manged to focus long enough to order something.

Working in the hotel industry all his life, Aiden encountered a larger than average number of people having sex in fairly public places. He wasn't a prude, but working in hotels meant having been the whoops, had no idea you all were using that fichus for cover person, a time too many. He worried too much about embarrassing employees who signed up only to serve and deliver food, not to be unwitting voyeurs.

But that did nothing to quell his, uh, imagination. Their food arrived. After a few bites, he put down his utensils. "Well, we could either talk about the weather, or I could tell you a few of the fantasies, I've worked up while we've been sitting here. Your choice."

Lulu pulled her fork slowly out of her mouth, and said, "Oh, let's go fantasies, please."

Between bites of food, they whispered in each others ears, about increasingly erotic things they wanted to do to each other, with and without the use of some of the food on the table. It became almost like sexual chess, he would whisper a suggestion about the syrup, she would counter with a suggestion involving the champagne. He shifted in his seat, this was either the best or worst idea he'd ever had.

When the waiter came and asked if they wanted to see the dessert menu they declined. Figuring out how he was going to get up and follow her out of this restaurant was a challenge. He didn't want to lose any of the delicious sexual tension they had built up together.

"Are you comfortable heading to my place next?" he asked once the waiter returned with their cards.

"Yes," she said.

They paused on the sidewalk outside the restaurant, lips and tongues meeting, as chests, hips and legs pressed deliciously, torturously together.

Lulu's phone chimed, and they broke apart to hop into the rideshare. Aiden was grateful for many things, the internet, syrup, condoms, but most of all, for this woman who appreciated both delicious fantasies, and also a little delayed gratification. But the time for delay was over.

Chapter 7

Lulu should be worried her panties might combust. She should also be a tiny bit worried that she was headed to a stranger's place, but Aiden didn't feel like a stranger anymore. She had texted his address to Maya, but she felt secure that what awaited her was orgasms.

His apartment was past a code box and a concierge. He swiped a key card in the elevator, and then led her quickly down the hallway, unlocking and leading her inside. She didn't look around as he shut the door. When he turned back, she pulled him down to kiss her, tasting him, trying to tell him with her tongue how much she wanted him.

She moved her hands down to his pants, undoing them and reaching into his boxer briefs. She stroked her hand along his cock, running her thumb across the tip. He hissed, and she gently released his cock, shimmying out of her panties, and popping open her purse to grab a condom. She placed the condom on his cock, slid her leg around his hip, and guided him inside, sighing as he pushed in.

"I have a bed, you know," he said, shifting his hands on her butt, to lift her a little, pushing him deeper inside.

"No time, come now, bed later," she said, tightening around him as he pumped in and out of her.

"Fair enough," he said. He shifted them so her back hit the wall, and she slid her other leg around his hip. His hands on her butt held her up as they moved together and apart, the friction and tempo speeding to a fever pace. She reached between them to stroke her clit and exploded. He pulsed and shuddered against her as he came, pressing her against the wall. After a moment she said, "Ready to let go?"

He pressed a kiss to her ear. "Yes ma'am." Reaching between them, he slowly helped her move back, and apart." He moved past her into the kitchen area, where he disposed of the condom.

She waited until he was back in front of her, to undo the top of her dress, releasing the side zipper and shimmying it off her naked body.

"Shall I leave the shoes on?" she asked.

His eyes raked her body, leaving her feeling tingly and hot, as if he hadn't just made her come delightfully.

"Yes, please," he said. "But I'm going to need a little recovery time."

"No problem. I can be patient," she said. "Why don't you show me around?" She pulled more condoms out of her purse, before placing the purse on top of her dress. He showed her the living room, with its large leather couch and equally large TV. She sat on the couch and decided to vamp it up a bit. "Ooh," she stroked her hand slowly across the cushion. "it feels like very fine leather." She watched Aiden's eyes darken as he looked at her. He had tucked himself back into his boxer briefs, and discarded the pants, but left his shirt on.

After the dining area and kitchen they found themselves in the bedroom. Lulu stripped off his shirt, folding it very carefully while he watched. She then slowly removed her shoes before climbing on to the bed. They went into the bedroom where he stripped off his briefs and climbed onto the bed. She had grabbed the condoms, slid one on him and then said, "Your fantasy this time."

He directed her to place her hands against the headboard, her butt sticking out behind. He moved behind her, reaching around to stroke her clit right before he pressed inside her.

She kept her arms braced over the head board, moving her hips with his as he pumped inside her. He kept one hand on her hip and the other played with her clit as they moved together. They moved faster, and he pressed the heel of his hand against her pubic bone and she came, shattering, tightening around him. He pumped inside her, increasing his pace, and she squeezed around him, and he shuddered and came.

Leaning a little harder against her back. He pressed a kiss to the nape of her neck and got up.

She slowly let go of the headboard, belatedly noting the ornate woodwork. She lay her head down on the pillow, wondering if this delightful fantastical orgasm man, might be too good to be true. But those were not good post-sex thoughts, so she pushed them away, leaving no hint of them as Aiden climbed back into bed with her. "Maybe a little rest before we finish the tour?" he said.

She nodded. "That couch is still on my list though."

"Everything is on my list," he said.

Chapter 8

Aiden's condo had become a mental flash book of sex with Lulu. The entryway, the dining room table, the bed of course, the couch, the shower, the kitchen counter, all of it.

He had intended to take her out for dinner, but they had instead gotten takeout. He was aware that eventually the realities of daily life would reassert themselves, and he would need to rediscover how to go three to four hours without regular sex.

This was bound to burn out, this constant need to come inside her, and to make her come.

This morning they had plans outside.

On the pretense of saving water, they had showered together, which had led to shenanigans on the bathroom counter. He would never be bored with this woman around, he wasn't sure he could maintain this level of sex, but he sure wanted to try.

Already, the idea of just fun with Lulu, didn't seem like enough. He wanted fun with her for sure, but he wanted more. But if she was just out of a relationship, he figured he wait until they'd spent more than a weekend together to ease her into that. Instead, he was going to take her to a museum. She'd never been to the Hirschhorn, and since it was one of his favorites in the Smithsonian, they were going. Sometimes the easiest way to convince someone of something wasn't to argue, it was to demonstrate.

He planned to demonstrate that they could be fun outside of sex.

They took metro down to the museum. He thought he heard her mutter the words vagina museum under her breath as they approached the building. He couldn't think of any way that asking her to clarify that would result in them getting kicked out of the museum. He held onto her hand as they wandered inside. On a Monday morning in September, most of the other visitors were tourists, backpacks, fanny packs, and souvenir t-shirts making them easy to spot. Perhaps having grown up in a large house with classical art had made him love the bold contemporary modern art on display in the Hirschhorn more. Or maybe he would always have loved it.

He had visited a few weeks ago, to check out the new New Media installation, so he led Lulu there first. Her dress today was a pattern that started off floral on one side and transitioned to check on the other, with pinks, reds, and purple throughout. He didn't know if she'd planned to look like a possible piece of modern art, or if it was a signal she'd enjoy this museum. One woman he'd brought here had, after they moved to the second floor, asked if there was any normal art.

He let go of her hand, wanting to let her move through the pieces at her own pace. "I hate it when people stand over me while, I do this," he said. "So I'll wander through the other way, and you can find me."

Lulu nodded, smiling at him, before turning back to the screen in front of her. He waved at the security guard he recognized from frequent visits. Twenty minutes later, he wondered if leaving Lulu was a mistake. What if she left? What if she was bored? What if she couldn't find him and thought he had left her? He knew, of course, she had a phone in her purse. He checked his, no texts or missed calls, so everything was fine. She was an adult, she wasn't even new to the city.

He found her near a set of windows, peering down at the courtyard talking on her phone. It was Monday, he reminded himself. Some people had work to attend to, and certainly he sometimes had to address something on what was supposed to be a day or evening off. He moved closer.

She gesticulated with the hand not pressed to her phone. "It's amazing. It's a great use of both video, text, and visuals. Remember the avant-garde fashion show, where all the models carried tablets with videos playing, it was like that, but it actually worked. We should take the interns at the Fashion Lab." She turned and saw him and smiled. "Okay, I found him, or he found me really. I'll talk to you later. Yes, tomorrow, I promise." She put her phone in her bag and leaned forward to kiss him, a quick kiss, full of joy and excitement.

"It was great," Lulu said. "Thank you for letting me go at my own pace. I got a thousand ideas, and when I couldn't find you right away, I called Maya to tell her about it before I forgot."

Aiden felt like a beam of sunshine had crawled across the floor and found him. Her excitement was infectious.

She grabbed his hand. "I know you've seen it, but let me show you this one again."

He followed her back into the exhibit area, barely glancing at the piece she stopped him in front of. He was content to listen to her talk about the color, the sound, and how they merged and inspired her. He had seen her in many moods, from wary, to sexy, to sated, but this one, this joy was his favorite.

He had planned a lunch for them elsewhere. The Hirschhorn only had a small cafe with snacks, but he sent an apologetic text cancelling it. They grabbed a quick drink and a pastry and walked through the rest of the museum together.

The day was sunny and mild, so they went out to the sculptures in the courtyard last. He found a good place to stand and watched as she took tons of photos.

She came and stood next to him, leaning into him. He put an arm around her waist. "Thank you. I know when I go into artiste mode, I can be a little much."

"Not at all. I'm glad you enjoyed it." His stomach growled and they both laughed.

"I guess I should feed you now." She pressed a quick kiss to his cheek before grabbing his hand and leading him out onto the sidewalk.

He had expected they would metro or rideshare somewhere with food. A number of the museums had cafes with more substantive menus, but the Mall and its immediate surroundings was not where most of the good food in DC was. But Lulu headed south, past government buildings, towards the smell of the river. The fish smell grew, as she led him towards a building with what looked like kitschy nineteen seventies style font, adorned with cartoon seafood.

She checked her phone. "Oh good, we missed the rush. You sit here. Any food restrictions?"

He shook his head. He sat at the small table and watched her move quickly along the stalls until he lost sight of her. He looked around. He had heard of the Fish Market of course. The internet existed, but good hotel staff also had suggestions and knowledge about the area to help guide customers. He had started as a front desk agent at the Union Camden. His parents had thought his dedication to starting there quaint.

Lulu came back with two soup containers and two paper bags. She placed everything on the table and then a stack of napkins. "Spoons!" She hopped up and raced back with two spoons. Handing him one, she used hers as a pointer. "Chowder," she indicated the tubs, "fried shrimp," she pointed to a bag, "And fried fish."

She popped open a soup tub and he did the same. It was delicious. Basic, but in the best way, as in it tasted like chowder, not deconstructed chowder, not a fancy spin on chowder, just chowder.

She reached into the bag and popped a fried shrimp in her mouth, making a small yum sound he felt in his bones.

He grabbed one for himself and had to groan too. She handed him a piece of fried fish with a smile and he opened his mouth letting her pop it in. It was salty and delicious and warm. He followed it with more chowder and in what felt like just a few minutes they had nothing but empty food containers.

"That was delicious, thank you."

"You're welcome," Lulu said. They stood, gathering up the stuff and taking it together to a trash can. Walking back outside they wandered further along the waterfront. In just a half block, the feel changed as they hit the newly redeveloped Wharf section. Shop signs with modern font and unusual punctuation dotted the lower half of a mix of hotel and condo space. Moving to the boardwalk stretch they held hands, as they walked along the river.

As they reached the part still under construction, she turned to him. "Did you have anything else on the plan for today or would you like to see my studio?"

Chapter 9

Lulu had brought other people to her studio. Studio was sort of a misnomer these days. In the early days, she and Maya had made everything themselves. Well, Lulu had since Maya was terrible with sewing more than a straight line. Later they had gotten big enough to justify having some fashion interns from the local art schools to help.

These days, she designed primarily on her laptop or tablet, sending images to the factory for mockups. She occasionally used her machine at home to try something out. But, she and Maya still used the first studio space in northeast DC that they had been able to afford. Just being there made her feel creative.

In addition to fashion interns and reporters, she had brought investors and family members to see the space. Nowadays investors were more likely to want to see the factory, to meet in conference rooms and have her bring drawings. Of course nowadays, more of the investors wanted to buy in to look cool. It was much easier to offer money or advice to a company that had been operating in the black for the last eighteen months. Much easier to offer distribution deals to a company that had been featured on red carpets and six seasons of this season's must haves. Yeah, once you were successful everyone wanted to help.

She fired off a quick text to Maya before they got on the metro. Maya was going to kill her for bringing an unexpected guest, but hopefully in the time it took them to switch lines and get there, Maya would be calmer.

She looked at Aiden. He looked so normal today, in his weekend clothes. The suit wearing version of him had been attractive, but the museum going, eating fried fish out of a paper bag version, this guy should have a warning label.

So, yeah, maybe taking him to the studio was another test. Could he be wonderful or would he try to share his fashion merchandising experience, gained from a lifelong experience of being, well, a man. Plenty of men, wearing ill-fitting suits, who didn't know the difference between a clutch and a tote, felt certain they knew how to run her business.

Lulu wasn't ready to give up this fun interlude, but she was trying to keep it just fun and nothing more.

Her phone beeped as they went above ground on the red line.

Maya: Haha.

Maya: Wait, are you serious?

Maya: Weren't you the one that made the no outsiders without warning rule? What if I was accounting naked?

She smiled at Aiden. "My business partner doesn't like surprises."

They moved off the train at Brookland. Aiden paused on the platform. "I don't want to mess things up, I can come see it another time."

Lulu didn't know how to tell him she needed him to see it now. Before she cracked and accidentally gave him a piece of herself. If he was just a fun interlude, none of this mattered, and they could bang each other until he got annoying or boring or both.

But if he was more than fun, she needed to know now, so she could shore up her armor and keep him out. More than fun always led to her curled up on the floor crying her eyes out, and she had a shoe business to launch. There was no time on the schedule for emotional breakdowns of the smushy heart kind.

So she smiled. "She'll adjust." She texted Maya from the escalator down to the street.

Lulu: Just a quick visit and I'll owe you the good ice cream. Plus, I can show you the pictures. See you in ten. Love ya!

She put the phone in her purse, and took Aiden's hand. The area around the metro had sprouted up with new buildings and shinier storefronts. A few blocks over, there were signs of change on the stretch LuWie was in too. The corner store and small chicken joint had closed down, one still vacant, the other replaced by a coffee shop. A glass door between the two, had a small sign and keycodes. The sign listed LuWie, a tailor who kept odd hours, and a computer repair shop.

Lulu led Aiden up the stairs to their shop.

The stylized L cupped the other letters on the door. She checked, Maya had unlocked the door. "Come on in."

They used to hire an intern to sit out front and look official on days they brought bigwigs through. Today the small podium behind the door was empty. Walking around the bamboo screens the rest of the space was open. Windows along the back wall showing a view of the back of the church on the other side of them. It let in enough sunlight to show off the hardwood floors. There was a small kitchenette on one end. A large table was in the center, where, Maya sat with her laptop. The other wall was mounted with early samples, and framed photos, along with a tablet, set to display a roving set of pictures.

"Hi, Maya, this is Aiden."

Maya stood and met Aiden partway as he moved towards her to greet her. They shook hands. "Hi, Maya. Sorry to barge in on you unexpectedly."

"Yeah, it's fine." Maya's tone was almost convincing enough for Lulu to buy it. She was really going to owe her the good ice cream. Like a whole gallon.

Lulu turned to ask Aiden if he wanted anything to drink. He had moved over to the wall, scanning the pictures, and pausing to watch the tablet cycle through.

"Do you need a drink, Aiden? We have water and seltzer."

"Water and water," Maya said softly, since she was of the opinion that offering water and seltzer as separate things was incorrect.

Aiden chuckled, looking back at Maya. "I'm fine. You two talk business, I can wait right here."

Maya gave an eyebrow raise that Lulu wasn't sure how to interpret. Lulu pulled out the photos, scrolling through them, with her phone out so both she and Maya could see. She grabbed the tablet from the table and started sketching off the idea for the multimedia show, to launch a line of modern inspired purses.

"Is this instead of or in addition to shoes?" Maya asked.

"In addition. But the shoes," Lulu paused as she envisioned it in her head. Their original plan had been to start with basic shoes, simple flats that folded up. Wearable but could also be tucked easily into a LuWie purse or clutch. They could do modern art inspired shoes too, shoes that coordinated with the new purses, but that would take longer.

"How about this, along with the standard colors we had planned on, if we did a limited edition patterned version. Super short run, like 200. For the rest, then we do the tagline, 'Shoes for when you want your purse to stand out.'"

"Can you sketch the shoe pattern for me right now?" Maya asked. "I can get on the phone with the factory and see what they think. They should be able to get us a cost estimate tomorrow, and a sample, well, soon, I hope. Plan B?"

"Plan B we just have the original shoes and start teasing a secret line of purses. I posted a picture from the museum."

"I saw that." Maya nodded. "I'll also check. Everything you're talking about sounds like we're clear in inspiration versus copy, but I'll talk to the suits."

"Oh, good point, thank you."

"Sketch." Maya tapped the tablet. "Then take this gentleman out of the office and go enjoy your day off. Ice cream tomorrow."

Lulu nodded, already drawing. She drew three and split the pages, so she could review them. Something was off. She pulled up a new page and tried again. Closer, but just...

"Picasso, gimme. You can noodle more tomorrow," Maya said gently pulling the tablet away from her. Lulu was going to protest that it was almost there, but saw from the light outside that they had been there longer than she had planned.

She turned to Aiden. He sat in a folding chair near the wall. Tapping away on his phone.

She moved over to him. "Sorry, I got a little caught up there."

He looked up and smiled. "No problem. Are you set? I can keep throwing birds at castles here." He showed her the new high score he gotten.

"I'm good. Thank you for being patient." She waved to Maya who was already on the phone with the factory. Aiden waved at her too.

Outside in the hallway, he slid an arm around her shoulder. "Thanks for letting me see that."

Lulu wasn't sure what she had expected from the visit to the studio. But Aiden him thanking her for letting him sit bored on a chair wasn't on the list at all.

"Well, I had planned to show you some of the photos and samples, not thrust you at our glory wall, and leave you while Maya and I worked."

"Glory wall?" Aiden stopped in the middle of the sidewalk, laughing so hard, he crouched down.

She wondered if he might drop all the way to the ground and roll around like the internet promised.

He was adorable when he laughed and if she wasn't so sure that somehow he was laughing at her, she would join in or hug him or something else ridiculous. Instead she waited for him to recover.

His laughter slowed and he stood back up. Looking at her expectant expression, he kissed her nose. "Sorry, I wasn't really laughing at you. Just glory wall is the perfect term for that. You know what a glory hole is, yes?" he asked.

Lulu felt her face heat, as she realized suddenly that's what Maya meant when she said that they couldn't call it that in front of the big investors, they'd get confused about who was screwing who. Maya was often making obscure references to TV shows and books Lulu either hadn't gotten to or hadn't read quite so many times as Maya, so usually she just rolled with it. But yes, she had heard of a glory hole, even though it was such a strange idea. You didn't hear stories of women — or men for that matter — setting up dildo walls. Although, now that she thought about it there were dildos with suction cups, so perhaps the answer was that people did do that.

Aiden kissed her again, probably to distract her, but it worked. His tongue, his taste, his hands pulling her tighter against him. She was well and truly distracted from whatever she had been thinking about that was not this man, that was not, more of this.

A siren went by, reminding her they were on a sidewalk, and they could be somewhere not outside.

She was gratified to notice Aiden's breathing had shifted to, proof they had distracted each other. "Takeout dinner at my place sound good?" he asked.

Lulu nodded, and they walked back to metro, hands linked. Her place was closer, but she wasn't ready for the image of him in more of her spaces. She could grab clothes on the way back to the studio tomorrow. Tonight she was going to stock up on fun.

Chapter 10

Aiden noticed Lulu was only half there. Maybe three quarters if he was fair. She smiled, she kissed him back when he kissed her, she agreed and made choices when he had offered choices for food. It wasn't just that she hadn't walked into his apartment and stripped in the doorway. Although, yes, he had realized a tiny part of him had hoped for a repeat performance, even if his thighs and forearms were grateful.

But she seemed distracted. Maybe she was still thinking about the design, somehow he thought it was something more. The food arrived, and they both ate and then packed up the rest.

"Hey," he said to her, closing the refrigerator door, "I have work tomorrow, but I'd love to do dinner tomorrow night. Either here or wherever."

"I'll have to see how it goes," Lulu said. "I may have to work late."

"I don't mind late dinner."

"I'll let you know." She kissed him then.

He knew she was distracting him from more questions, but her hands roamed his chest, and stroked lower and he forgot what he was worried about. He picked her up and carried her into the bedroom, grabbing a sleeve of condoms and putting them on the bed. He shucked his shoes, socks, and folded the pants. Lulu's clothes were already on the floor except the shoes. He sat her on the edge of the bed, and knelt down. He found the buckle on them and slipped each off, pressing kisses to the bottom of each foot. He slid his thumbs up the inside of her legs, shifting himself up, to spread the lips of her center wide, looking at her clit. He dipped his thumb inside her, sliding the moisture around her clit, looking up at her face before leaning in to suck her clit into his mouth while he pumped his thumb and forefinger inside her. Her breathing shifted as she moaned, and sensing she was close her sucked harder, curling his finger inside her. She spasmed and came, and he ran his tongue gently across her center. He stood, and removed his boxers, sliding the condom on. He leaned forward and waited until she looked at him. "Ready?" he asked.

"Please, now," she said.

He hooked her legs over his and guided himself inside her, pushing slowly. Grasping her hips, he began thrusting. She tipped her pelvis and met his thrusts. He felt his body grow tighter, harder, he could feel it in his spine and shifted trying to get the angle that would help her come too. Lulu pinched her nipples and shuddered around him, tightening pulsing. He tried to hold on, to feel each of her pulses before he let go. But he shuddered and came, feeling pulses he could no longer identify the origin of.

After a moment, he moved back to dispose of the condom. Lulu lay where he left her, legs still dangling over the edge. He shifted her up, so he could join her on the bed. He pulled her to him, stroking over her chest, her hips, trying to memorize the texture of every piece of her.

As he fell asleep with her naked in his arms, he tried to tell himself the arm around her was because he wanted to keep her warm, and not because he was afraid without it she would disappear.

Chapter 11

Aiden was clearly a morning person. He moved out of bed the second his phone buzzed and returned with two coffee mugs. He had put milk in hers and as Lulu sat on his bed and sipped it. It was pretty good coffee too. He was partially dressed when she felt she had sipped enough to get up and find out what kind of schedule they were working with. She just had to throw her clothes back on, but she usually liked to work her morning in stages.

Lulu should have left last night but had been unable to resist the option of sleeping next to him. Aiden was so warm, and she usually slept under blankets even in the dead of summer. He had pants on and his shirt half buttoned.

"You can stay for a bit, if you want," he said. "I need to be in by nine today, but you don't have to leave just because I am."

Lulu didn't want to stay in his place where she might do something ridiculous like try to sniff his suit closet, so she shook her head.

"No, I can be ready. How much time do we have?" she asked.

"Twenty minutes," he said.

He was half dressed and he still had twenty minutes?

She put her coffee down next to the bed, grabbed a condom, and smiled watching his fingers pause on his shirt buttons. "Did you say twenty whole minutes?" She stood and licked his ear in case her meaning wasn't clear.

Several very satisfying moments later, she rubbed spot on his collarbone that she had scraped with her teeth. The marks were disappearing already. "So, I guess I should get dressed now," she said.

"You are dangerous when naked, so probably so," he said, kissing her nose. He went to dispose of the condom. She gathered up her clothes, and threw them on. She likely reeked of sex, but she couldn't find it in her to care. Leaving together, even if she was headed home first, felt almost domestic.

Lulu kissed him goodbye on the metro, she needed to go north, rather than south, and promised to call if she could do dinner. She was pretty sure she should take an Aiden break and focus on her business. The part of her life that was so much more likely to work out. Time with him was dangerous, even if it had led to an impressive amount of orgasms.

But as she stepped into her place she wondered what kind of coffee he had given her. She should get some. Maybe that was what helped make mornings more bearable.

MAYA LOOKED UP IN SURPRISE when Lulu walked in with ice cream. "You're here very early."

"You're here," Lulu said. Sure, their factory was on the west coast, so Lulu often took advantage of that and strolled in a little closer to ten. She worked late, and partied later, and since partying was brand building too, it all worked out.

"Yes, but I like being here before everyone else," Maya said.

"I can leave and come back."

"Not with that ice cream you can't. Gimme!" Maya moved towards her, taking one of the pints out of her arms. The small fridge in their kitchenette had an oddly shaped freezer, they'd discovered pint containers fit in there better than gallons. So, Lulu had brought four pints, each in a different flavor.

"Wow," Maya said, "you really felt bad. Or did something else. Oh my god, you're here with terrible news aren't you?"

"Nope, no terrible news," Lulu said. "I couldn't decide if we needed Brave Vanilla or Luscious Lemon more, so I got both."

"And also Cake Me and Chocolate Diva."

Lulu shrugged. "Good complementary flavors." Reaching in to her bucket style purse, she grabbed the bottle of whipped cream.

"Ah yes, healthy breakfast." Maya clapped her hands together in glee. She grabbed bowls and spoons from the cabinet and brought them over, moving her laptop to the chair so it was out of range. Lulu grabbed a bowl, and they each began spooning ice cream chunks into their bowls. Lulu had a good scoop of each flavor before she topped it with whipped cream.

She handed the bottle to Maya who topped her bowl and then held the bottle up, "Shots?"

"Shots."

Maya squirted a dollop of whipped cream into her mouth before handing the bottle back to Lulu who did the same.

Lulu placed her purse on the table, and took a picture of the purse with their bowls. "I'll post it later, let's eat." She pulled up a chair and Maya grabbed another one, so she didn't have to disturb her laptop.

"So, that guy yesterday, he's not an investor, right?"

"No, we're just having fun."

Maya raised her eyebrows at her. "And you brought him here because?"

"I just wanted him to see." Lulu took a large bite, making sure to get enough whipped cream on the spoon.

"You wanted him to see what? We didn't have any samples here, no fashion interns scrambling to look busy, no new season look books, none of the things we normally show people."

"I just, I wanted to see what he would say," Lulu said. It sounded silly even to her ears. She was usually great at double speak, at schmoozing and making things sound bigger, more important, or more whatever than they were. But she didn't know how to explain this to Maya. She could barely explain it to herself.

"Was he supposed to be impressed or unimpressed? What does he do?"

"He works in a hotel."

"Doing?"

Lulu shrugged. "Not sure."

"So, let me recap. You dumped Richard. You get on a train. You meet a guy. You bring him here, which usually we don't do, but you haven't asked what he does? Did you at least google him?"

"No."

"Oh my god, Lulu." Maya put her spoon down. "How do you know he's not married, or has kids, or I don't know, tries to find accessories moguls on the train to steal their ideas?"

"I'm pretty sure he didn't know I'm an accessories mogul." He hadn't asked any weird questions, not even when she brought him to the studio.

"What is his name?" Maya put down her spoon and grabbed her laptop.

"Aiden."

"Last name?"

Lulu shrugged, embarrassed. This was a good reminder. They were just having fun. Aiden probably didn't know her last name either. He knew where she worked so with half a second and google he could figure it out. "He works at the Union Camden. I have his address too."

"You think you have his address since you would have no way of verifying that, or even that that's his only address." Maya typed forcefully on her laptop. "Wait, this guy? Oh, well," Maya tapped more. "Yeah, his bio does not mention a family, but have you ever noticed dude's bios hardly ever mention their family if they have one and ladies bios almost always do. And well, I don't have enough data on agender and non-binary folk to assign them a statistical likelihood yet.

"He participated in a charity bachelor thing last year, so as of last year he wasn't married. And is this the address you went to?" Maya tipped the screen to her.

There were four windows open, a business headshot from the Union Camden website listing Aiden as the hotel manager, a photo from a charity gala where he was in a tux , an address that was the apartment she'd been at this morning, and a listing putting him on the board of directors for a pet shelter. Lulu was going to need to google the tux picture later for reasons. "Yeah, that's the one." She felt itchy. Maya had found this in seconds of googling. Heck, Maya probably knew people at the pet shelter she could ask about Aiden.

Lulu didn't always operate on the assumption that people were lying to her, but this was some basic stuff she should have asked him. Not, are you on a charity board, because, well, that one wasn't normal.

Aiden didn't appear to have lied about, well, anything. If she had assumed worked in a hotel meant worked in a hotel, not managed the entire hotel, well, that was her fault for not prying further. Part of her liked that he hadn't made a huge deal about it. He seemed kind of young to be a manager of an entire hotel, but she had never actually met a manager of a whole hotel. And since she had appeared on two thirty under thirty lists in the last year, she wasn't sure why he couldn't also have worked his way up from wherever he had started.

"So basically he was just who he said." She handed the laptop back to Maya.

"You know I worry." Maya set the laptop back down and returned to her ice cream.

"I know, and I appreciate that. But it doesn't matter he's just fun." Just fun she reminded the Lucinda voice that told her Maya was saying the same things it had been trying to tell her. If Aiden had turned out to be married or a fast food worker with a key to a fabulous apartment, it wouldn't have mattered. They could still go to museums, and eat delicious food, and have amazing sex. These things only mattered if they had a future, but he was a rebound, so they didn't. They were just for now.

Time to focus on her real future. Her job. Her company. The stuff you could count on.

Chapter 12

Rhian poked her head in Aiden's office. "Just a heads up, we might need to use your name in vain tonight."

"Okay," he said. "Normal or late check in, do we think?"

"They didn't ask for late check in, so it may be while you're still here. In which case we'll let you know to slip out the back."

"If it gets tense, I can jump in." The joy of being listed as the hotel manager on the website, was guests with special requests often googled and demanded him by name if their requests were not handled to their liking. One of the policies they had in place was that staff on duty were allowed to run things one rung up and claim it had been approved or denied by him. He asked for some of those things to be emailed to him, so he could pretend to remember if it came up if he met the guest somewhere. In most cases, the listing he got every week contained people he never did run into again. A few folks who attended some of the same charity functions that his grandmother and parents supported. Often exactly the kind of pancake situation he had thought of when he first met Lulu, so he only attended a few of those each year. But Rhian was skilled at identifying guests that might fall into such a category.

"I'm hoping you won't need to," Rhian said. "But I'll let you know."

"Okay." He turned back to his computer. But now that he had thought of pancakes and Lulu, he was unable to focus on the proposal for the ballroom redesign in front of him.

He tried to decide which dinner option would be most irresistible to her. She had selected a trendy brunch place, had enjoyed takeout, had happily munched museum pastries, and knew her way around a fish market. She clearly knew her way around fashion and accessories, and yet, hadn't seemed to care weather he wore a suit or chinos. It was possible she was mostly perfect. She snored a little, but it was adorable. Oh, and she just wanted fun. Aiden had forgotten that part.

Well, what counted as fun dinner? Inspired, he texted her, grabbing a picture from the fondue place's website. He hoped the combination of the visual and obviously, the opportunity to have dinner with him would do the trick. He put the phone down so that he couldn't stare at the text bubble waiting to see when she responded. She was working. So, the time it took her to respond was meaningless. Probably.

His phone buzzed.

Lulu: What time?

Aiden smiled. Aiden: Six thirty? I can meet you at your office.

Lulu: No need. You're closer. I can meet you at the hotel.

Dinner, she was having dinner, with him. The more than fun part he would worry about later.

Aiden: Okay, looking forward to it.

He hit send and then wanted to smack himself. He sounded like a corporate message. We really appreciate your dedication to us and look forward to more in the future. Whatever, he was better in person, and good thing he was going to get to see her tonight to remind her.

Chapter 13

Lulu had posted the ice cream and purse photo to the company's social media with the caption, "How we celebrate new things on the horizon at LuWie HQ". The first comments had all been excitement, questions about what kind of ice cream, and of course a couple folks commenting that ice cream was unhealthy and they should stop. Lulu resisted sending those folks a picture of her with a mouth full of ice cream. Overall, a pretty decent ratio.

A few comments appeared speculating that they were branching off into shoes. Not surprising, it had been a common request. Their purse manufacturer didn't have the capacity to make shoes, equipment differences. Maya and Lulu had done lots of research, wanting to stick with American factories. Some of them they'd already tried, and hadn't been happy with the purses, so for sure weren't going back to see if the shoes were different.

The initial samples they'd gotten from this place had been excellent. Exactly what they were going for, and the price quote was great too. Lulu had been excited then the delivery person arrived this morning with the new pattern sample.

At least until she opened the box. "Maya," she said.

Maya walked over and they both stared at the sample.

The fabric was different. That happened sometimes with samples, especially rush ones. The flat itself was a different shape, with a round toe rather than pointy, and the sole itself lacked the flexibility to bend. Lulu grabbed a purse sample they had in the studio and tried folding the shoe into it. The seam between the sole and the shoe upper split.

She and Maya called the factory, hoping this was a small thing. Perhaps the patterned fabric had different capabilities. Or they had thought she meant a different style not the same style with a patterned upper.

But a day's worth of conference calls and video chats later, Lulu had the beginnings of a low grade headache. She put the two shoes — the original samples and the new one in front of the camera — to demonstrate how different they were. The manager she and Maya had signed all the contracts with had been in a car accident. She was expected to recover, but in the interim her son had taken over. And he felt the quote they'd been given based on the materials of the prior samples was incorrect. So the new sample was all they could reasonably provide at the quote.

When Maya had dug out the contracts, including the sign off of the specific samples, he, his name was Everett, had argued there was a clause in there for equivalents if there was a change in material availability. Lulu was thinking of breaking out her sewing machine to make a pin cushion with his face on it tonight.

Of course there was a clause, but, Lulu had reminded him it required sign off from them. Apparently he considered this inferior shoe, a sign off.

Maya jumped up from her chair and came back from the fridge with the cake ice cream and the whipped cream.

She handed Lulu a spoon and Lulu realized she probably needed to eat something not in the ice cream family today. Oh no. "Crap." She grabbed her phone.

"Crap, indeed," Maya said.

"Oh, that too, I just realized I was supposed to meet Aiden for dinner."

"Go," Maya waved with the hand not spooning ice cream, "there's nothing else we can do here. You know, except eat ice cream."

"Well, but we need to decide..." she trailed off. Maya was right. They'd talked it to death, between their calls with Everett and his team. They could cancel the contract but that would mean starting again finding a manufacturer who could work within their price point and get the fabrics and specs they wanted. They wouldn't be able to use the samples they had. They still had all the sketches to work with, but sharing the samples one factory made, while planning to end their contract, would put them in breach.

So basically, there were no good choices. Even trying to get a new price point from Everett for the original design was fraught, anyone who would do this was not a good business partner. They could hope Everett's mom returned and agreed to the originals. But that would put them in limbo for possibly months, assuming she did come back and not take early retirement.

They already knew they were cancelling the contract. And they'd need that taken care of before they began the search for a new manufacturer, to avoid — as much as they could — getting a reputation for being backstabbing designers. So the shoe launch was on hold, they were going to miss being able to time it with the fall fashion weeks. LuWie didn't have an official fashion tent for such things, but they had hoped to plant a few folks wearing the shoes in the crowd to build buzz. Stage a rogue show with the shoes somewhere else. It wasn't the end of the world, but it sucked. It sucked a lot.

Tomorrow at least she could send design or two to their purse manufacturer and get that moving.

"Crazy day," she texted Aiden. "I'm running late, but I'm on my way. Did we need to worry about making a reservation?"

Lulu kind of wanted to go home and have real food on her couch and catch up on some streaming. But, unlike some people named Everett, she lived up to the promises she made.

Aiden: I'm sorry you had an odd day. I will check with the restaurant, but if they can't be flexible, I can. Let me know when you arrive.

She tossed her stuff in her bag. Looking at Maya she said, "Promise me you are going to eat real food. I will call delivery now if I need to."

"Yeah, yeah, I'll pick up stuff on the way home. I'll be right behind you. Also, ice cream is real food."

Lulu nodded. "You are correct. I apologize to the ice cream for besmirching it."

"Besmirch is a good word for today."

Lulu sighed. She leaned over and hugged Maya. "Thank you for being my best business partner I'd ever want to have to deal with this mess."

"Right back atcha, lady. Go meet your funfetti man."

Lulu giggled. He was like funfetti, surprisingly enjoyable. It was nice to have a thing to look forward to after a bad day at work.

Chapter 14

Rhian: Aiden, please stay out of the lobby. You are in a very important corporate meeting right now.

Aiden: Okay. I'll let Kyran know to send my friend back when she arrives.

Rhian: Another special room needing friend?

Aiden smiled at the phone. She definitely wasn't that worried about the guest then, which was reassuring.

Aiden: Aren't you handling an important issue right now? But no, no rooms needed tonight.

Sure the idea of recreating their hotel room magic appealed, all except for the part where his co-workers continued to make comments. Besides, he'd rather go to his apartment, or maybe go to her place. Of course, if he was trying to prove they were more than just fun, perhaps he should try to go twenty-four hours without having sex with her. Nope, that seemed like a terrible idea. He was better off proving not only fun. As in sex and other things.

Rhian: I'm going down, but you should stay upstairs, or use the back way.

Kyran: Your friend is here, but there's an issue.

"I'm coming with you," he texted Rhian after letting Kyran know he'd be right down.

"Why are you coming with me after we discussed this?" Rhian asked as they got in the elevator.

"My friend is here. So let's just get everything solved fast. What do you know?"

Rhian gave him a succinct rundown. A regular guest of many of the Camden hotels, the customer file indicated he usually requested a king-size room, and then waited until he arrived to demand an upgrade to a suite. Currently their suites were booked solid, so that wasn't an option. They had planned to offer a champagne bottle sent to the room, which was a nice room with a view of some of the monuments. The guest was throwing around words like friend of the Camden family and regular guest, and various other combination threats and veiled implied connections. The other guests in line had all been swiftly processed and offered a free bottle of wine from room service.

The elevator doors opened and he spotted Lulu immediately, her brightly colored dress standing out against the navy of Kyran and the other hotel employee — Jo. A man with dark hair in a dark suit hand his hand on Lulu. Everything about her posture said she wanted if off, and the dark red of the man's face suggested whatever he was saying wasn't happy. Rhian touched his arm. "Please stay here and let us solve this, or at least let us send him to you."

"Thirty seconds to get Lulu away from him," Aiden said.

Rhian nodded. Aiden tried to breathe deeply and smile. Looking around the lobby the staff had done a great job of getting people to either move to their rooms, or into the bar. He knew Lulu was a capable woman, and he knew Kyran and Jo and Rhian would do their best to de-escalate. Him showing up would likely escalate things. And it would shift the dynamic enough that it might look to any other guest coming onto the scene like they were bullying guests. He was better staying here even though he hated it.

The man's arm tugged Lulu and she pushed back against his chest. Jo stepped closer and he dropped his hands, holding them in the air, the picture of oh but I am so harmless.

Aiden had to relax his jaw before he cracked a tooth. But he knew that was progress. It meant the man, the guest he reminded himself, had recognized the optics and was shifting into I'm such a good guy mode. This was the hardest part of customer service, not being nice to jerks, Aiden found himself well-trained for that. No, it was pretending that of course they didn't really think things were that bad, of course they misunderstood this man's intent when he grabbed another guest.

Kyran took a step back. Rhian pointed towards Aiden, and Lulu nodded in a way that didn't seem happy, more resigned. The man offered his arm to Lulu. She started walking as if she hadn't noticed and he followed. They went past Aiden into the bar.

Rhian and Jo came to Aiden, "She's agreed to talk to him for a few minutes in the bar," Rhian said. "I'm going to alert the staff to keep any eye on them, but I think he's calmed down enough. We have agreed he can continue to stay here if there are no further incidents. He, well, we'll talk more about some of the things he said tomorrow. Jo, you were doing a great job with him, no way to know that seeing Ms. Williams was going to," she glanced at Aiden, "escalate things. Great job, please make sure to document things."

Jo nodded. She went back to the front desk.

Rhian looked at Aiden. "I'm going to suggest that you go back to your office and I can bring Lulu to you the second she and our guest are done. You lurking there isn't conducive to anything."

Aiden pushed away from the wall. Rhian's suggestion made sense, he just felt itchy. But lurking between the hotel elevators and the bar entrance was not a good look for anyone, so he should at least move. Lulu walked out of the bar muttering, "And this is why I don't date billionaires." She paused and looked around spotting him and Rhian.

She stepped to him. "Hi, Aiden, I would like to go please."

Aiden stepped forward and offered her his hand. She grabbed it, and they had gone three steps, when Aiden heard, "Oh, come on, this guy?"

Aiden was willing to keep going, betting he wouldn't follow them out of the hotel, but Lulu stopped. "Get over it, Richard. Or don't. You don't get a say in my life."

Richard shook his head, "Fine, but let's not pretend you're rediscovering simplicity or whatever. Just own that you are trading up, Lucinda. You ditched me for another billionaire."

Lulu glanced at Aiden, then back at Richard. "Richard, stop making scenes." She turned back around and moved towards the hotel entrance, but Aiden noticed the second they were on the sidewalk she dropped his hand. "I've had a really long day. Maybe we should...not."

"Have you eaten?" he asked. Aiden got the sense that not only had they stopped being fun, but that they each had a lot of questions. He hoped the answers would get them past this, but he was feeling sticky. He felt like he was trying to ignore a piece of gum stuck to his shoe and walk normally even though one foot kept sticking to the floor.

"No."

"I know a place that's close." He led her a few blocks away, feeling gratified when she let him hold her hand. They recommended this place to couples who wanted somewhere to eat where they could actually hear each other talk. He smiled at the hostess who recognized him and led them to a table in the corner.

The lighting was dim, each table had a small candle. They ordered drinks and food from the waitress who came over quickly. And then he looked back at Lulu. She was gorgeous in the candle light, sitting in her chair, fidgeting with her napkin. He hoped, really hoped, she wasn't about to ditch him too.

Chapter 15

Lulu's hopes for the evening had involved food and stress relief. Instead she'd managed to run into a crabby ex, and it looked like maybe her fling was just another entitled dude too. Maya might be right, she should research her flings better. Or ditch them faster, not fall for the food, the museum trips, the lack of mansplaining. These were basic things. She had made them out to be bigger and more important than they needed to be, instead of cutting things off after a night or two and moving on.

But she did need food. And if the stress relief that lay ahead of her was ditching another dude, so be it.

"So, yeah," Lulu said, "Richard is my ex, and he didn't used to be that guy who caused scenes, but I guess today he did."

The waitress dropped bread on the table and Lulu grabbed a piece. If she ended up storming out of here before the fish she'd ordered had arrived, she needed sustenance.

"You are not responsible for Richard's behavior."

Lulu knew that, but was pleased to hear Aiden did too. She also wanted him to know the hotel employees had done their best to keep everyone calm. "Kyran was trying to lead me, I guess up to your office, when Richard spotted us. The other lady, Jo, she tried to distract him, but Richard can be very focused." It was great when the focus was let's give Lucinda a memorable night out. It was less great when he was focused on being at all the fundraisers, being seen at all the places, or when he needed to review the list of celebrity attendees before he would attend a protest.

He hadn't been an awful boyfriend, but there were things that happened to be true about a lot of people born into so much privilege.

It wasn't that they didn't know how to work hard or take risks, it was that they didn't understand what it meant for those risks to carry real consequences. And so, in Lulu's experience, relationships with billionaires stalled out faster.

"I'm glad to hear that," Aiden said, "but are you okay?"

"I'm fine." She glanced at Aiden and tried to figure out his mood. He seemed off. But not in a clear way. He didn't seem angry to find out she had an ex. He didn't seem jealous. And he didn't seem pleased to have walked away with her in front of his supposed rival. But while his concern felt genuine, he also didn't seem to be asking because he was worried tonight wasn't going as planned, although it clearly wasn't.

"So, do you prefer Lucinda?" Aiden asked.

Not where Lulu would have started, but sure. "My birth name is Lucinda Wei Williams. But Lulu, while yes, technically a persona I created, is me. Lulu's social media version of her life is grander, but it's still me. So, no I worked hard to be Lulu, I could have worked just as hard to be known as Lucinda if I wanted to."

"Okay. And I guess, since it occurs to me we skipped over that, I should explain I'm Aiden Camden George."

The waitress arrived with their plates. They leaned back to create space for her to slide their food in. Lulu smiled at her and took a quick bite.

She looked across at Aiden. Aiden Camden George. Had she been so distracted by the suit that she hadn't noticed that? No. He had just been listed on the site as Aiden George. Had Lulu been less distracted she might have remembered what that meant. The Camden family were longtime residents of the area, the growing hotel chain headquarters were located nearby. They had had a daughter who married a non-billionaire gentleman named George. This had happened well before Lulu and she supposed Aiden had been born. But was still alluded to in some of the fancy magazines that now found LuWie a worthy business to cover.

And now Richard's stupid comment started to make sense. She had leapt out of the frying pan into the fire.

Lulu took two more bites of fish.

"So, are you a billionaire?" she asked.

"No. I mean my grandparents have done very well, and my family, but me personally, no."

Lulu gave Aiden credit. Usually folks tried to claim all their family's accomplishments. "Do you have siblings?" she asked.

"No. Do you?" he answered. His tone was short, indicating he knew this conversation wasn't as friendly as the words suggested. Well, the man worked in a customer service business. It was good that he had such instincts.

"I do. One brother. He's a teacher. Do you have cousins?" she asked.

"Several, do you want a list?"

"Not now, thanks. And, is your mother the Camden?"

"Yes," he answered, his tone bored.

Lulu was bored too. Bored with men who thought being from money wasn't interesting. It wasn't as interesting as many of them thought it was, but it was still important.

"And so, if I recall correctly that means you are the direct line, since the founding Camden's had only one child, yes?"

"Yes."

"So when you say you're not a billionaire, you mean, not yet. Cool. This has been fun." Lulu placed her napkin and silverware on the table. "Bye." She walked out, pausing to hand money to the hostess to share with the server. She imagined Aiden was too kind to blame the servers for a bad evening, but she wanted to be sure. She went quickly around the corner, criss-crossing, and jaywalking across the streets. She needed blocks between her and that hotel, her and that man, her and any stupid man.

Lulu got to metro before the tears hit. She wiped her face carefully, trying to dab her eyes without smearing anything. Damn eye makeup.

She placed an order for pizza while she waited for the train. She was going to need all the sustenance for tomorrow.

Chapter 16

Aiden had met plenty of people who oohed and ahed at the Camden connection. He had gotten used to saving it, keeping his ties to the family, even while he worked in the family business, under wraps.

When dating, folks either got very excited, a little too excited. And then bored when they realized that he wasn't rich, not at least at the jet setting around the world standards they often imagined. Since the only way he was going to theoretically become crazy rich was if his grandparents passed away, he wasn't in any hurry for that to happen.

So, Lulu dumping him because he was too rich was new. He had slept badly last night, his apartment still full of Lulu ghosts that dogged him at every turn.

Marcus poked his head in. "So I hear you caused a commotion in the lobby."

"You need better sources," he said keeping his eyes on the computer monitor in front of him. He tabbed back to the plans from the customer database he had not been misusing. It technically wasn't misuse to look at the history of a customer he had personally witnessed causing a commotion in the lobby.

Ah, good, he couldn't even think the word commotion without thinking of Lulu.

Richard's customer history before yesterday was as Rhian had said. While big on the last minute room upgrade, he seemed to work on charm. He had never so much as spoken a terse word to a bartender. So basically, Richard was a generally well-behaved guest who had gotten a little out of it when confronted with an ex.

"So, you didn't go down to the lobby after Rhian suggested you stay away, because a guest was getting into it with your special friend?"

Aiden didn't have to look at Marcus to know he had made air quotes around the words special friend.

"I came down to check on my friend who was here to see me," Aiden said. "I did not interfere, not even when he grabbed her."

"Wait, he got physical with her?" Marcus stepped into the office. "And he's still staying here?"

Aiden shook his head. "He didn't hurt her. Jo and Kyran were right there. He was just trying to talk to her." And now Aiden was in the unenviable position of sympathizing with the jerk. Guest not jerk. Wanting to talk to Lulu when she didn't want to talk to you was a feeling he had become familiar with. She had moved so swiftly out of the restaurant. He'd thrown heaping amounts of cash on the table and raced out after her, but he hadn't been able to find a trace of her. No sign of her brightly colored dress making it's way down the street. He didn't know where she lived, only where she worked, and showing up at her office this morning had been tempting, but maybe she was right. Maybe they had just been fun, and any images he'd had of a future for the two of them were just fantasies on his part.

He could find someone to date that both wasn't after his money but also didn't hate it. Besides, hating money when you owned a retail business that appeared to be on track to make oneself a multimillionaire was a little hypocritical. And Aiden hated hypocrites. He certainly didn't want to continue dating them or even just smell them one last time.

"So you watched a guest get handsy with your special friend and let Kyran and Jo handle it? I guess you are more evolved than I."

Aiden knew Marcus was needling him. But that reminded him of something. Against his better judgment, he opened a new tab in his internet browser and googled their guest. It didn't take long for the search results to help him find a picture of Lulu and Richard, wearing the dress he remembered from the train, the dress he had helped her peel off in this very hotel. The caption indicated they were at a fundraiser for a museum in New York. So that was the pancake she had been at. So yeah. He was just a little fun for her. Nothing more.

Chapter 17

Lulu could barely remember what day of the week it was. They had initiated the termination clause in their contract with their now former shoe manufacturer. A meeting with their lawyer had assured them that whatever threats the manufacturer made, since they had changed the materials and had not gotten approval, LuWie Inc was within their rights to cancel the arrangement. They had shipped back the samples and while Lulu missed those original ones, it was simpler.

When she and Maya had talked to their purse plant about some of the new designs, they had mentioned they were looking into buying a nearby shoe manufacturer. It was one that Maya and Lulu had had on their list to check out, after things fell through. And if it meant they could continue working with a group already committed to mutually successful arrangements, so much the better. It would still be for the spring fashion weeks, rather than fall. Since the spring fashion weeks were when fall and winter looks debuted, she had sketched up a pair of boots to go with the flats. If they could rely on laces to maintain the structural integrity, they could possibly create a boot that also folded up pretty flat. Not as flat as the flats, but flat enough to go with a few cute dresses and sweaters into a weekend bag she had also recently finished the design for.

"Go home," Maya said, tugging on the tablet in Lulu's hands.

"I'm almost done." She tugged back. It was a little wristlet, big enough to hold a phone and other essentials. She had this idea that instead of a bracelet band it could have a cuff, with laces to match the boots. It would be an incredible look. She was going to need to break out the sewing machine to see if this was even possible before she tried to explain it to the factory. She could also try braiding it to look like a strap for a more everyday look.

"Lulu, do you have food at home?"

She waved a hand in dismissal at Maya before returning her finger to the tablet. She sketched out the idea, first with a laced arm cuff style, and then, saving and opening a new sketch page, braided. It didn't always lead to success, but when the sketch looked good, Lulu felt better about the prospects.

"Hit save before I yank it out of your hands," Maya said.

She hit save, but clutched the tablet to her body. "I'm going." Looking up she realized it was fully dark outside. She checked the date display on the tablet. It was Saturday. That didn't seem right. Oh wait, the lawyer had agreed to make time for a quick meeting on Saturday since things were urgent. That had been at three though.

She hugged Maya. "Sorry, I know you have other things to do than babysit me."

Maya flicked off the lights, and handed Lulu her bag.

As they walked outside, Maya asked again. "Is there food in your apartment?"

"Of course," Lulu said, even though she wasn't sure if she had things that weren't cereal. But cereal was food.

"Yeah, I'm coming home with you," Maya said, steering them to metro.

"Don't you have awesome Saturday night plans?" Lulu asked.

"You say this like dinner with my bestie while we watch TV or maybe share details about billionaires we have bedded isn't a great plan."

"We are not watching any procedurals. No dead bodies, real or fake," Lulu said as they got onto the train.

"Okay, but I get to pick the delivery place," Maya said.

"Deal," Lulu said.

Maya picked Thai and they settled on the couch with the food. Lulu could see her sewing machine sitting at the small table next to her and wanted to grab some sample fabric and get going. But time with Maya, especially non-work time, had been in short supply of late. Besides, she was going to need to hit up the local fabric store. She had some of what she needed, but definitely not enough lacing for what she wanted to try. She could shred some leather though.

"Hello." Maya waved her fork in Lulu's face.

"What?" Lulu asked.

"So, I told my banged a billionaire story, now it's your turn."

"Wait, you did?" Lulu was sure she hadn't missed that much.

"I'll send you the link to the fanfic. It's me and Emma Frost the White Queen."

"Isn't she cold and, well, pointy?" Lulu was not an expert in the superheroes.

"Only in some forms," Maya said. "So, your turn."

"Trading fanfic for actual stories is not exactly equitable."

"Au contraire. Some people draw or sew, I create with words. So, spill. This just fun dude you brought to our office for no reason that now has you throwing yourself into your work and running yourself ragged turned out to what — be another boring billionaire?"

Lulu nodded although the annoying Lucinda voice was back. Fine, Aiden hadn't been boring, but he would have been. So it was good she had left. Good she had cut things off. Good she hadn't heard from him at all.

"But the sex was good?" Maya asked.

"It was." Lulu's face smiled before she could stop it. Getting food with him had been enjoyable to. Talking with him on the train, going to the museum, all of it. It seemed impossible that she had only known him a matter of days and had learned so many things about him. But of course they had missed all the normal things, missed exchanging last names, and jobs, and family wealth history. So, it was the closest equivalent to a vacation fling one could have with someone that had apparently grown up only six miles away. But an important six miles.

He had gone to fancy prep schools while she had attended public schools in three different school districts. He had gone to a fancy university, and she had gotten a scholarship to cover her state tuition. They had lived lives that were geographically near, but as far apart as could be. That she showed up on fancy lists now, did nothing to close that gap.

"Have you called, texted, or social media stalked?" Maya asked.

"No," Lulu drew out the word.

"Why don't I believe you?"

"Is Wikipedia social media? Hey, that rhymes?" And suddenly the memory of commotion and locomotion popped into her head. Damnit. How had he gotten all over her brain?

"Normally, I would say no, since most of us don't have Wiki pages."

"You're on wiki," Lulu said. They both were. There was a page on the company and one on Lulu. It listed her real name too, because like Richard, Wikipedia liked to share government names with folks.

"I'm quite happy to be basically a footnote in your Wikipedia page. So, this wiki stalking, did we learn anything interesting?"

"No. He doesn't have his own page."

"So, help me out here. Should I find out if we can get ice cream and whipped cream delivered, so we can commiserate over one more boring billionaire? Or am I supposed to be encouraging you to not let other boring billionaires let you toss away a possibly good guy too soon? I can go either way, I just can't tell where we are."

"Yeah. Wait, you can get ice cream delivered?" Lulu asked.

"Of course you can. You can get practically anything delivered."

"You liked him, right?"

Maya looked carefully at Lulu, like she was afraid Lulu was fragile. Lulu did her best to look strong and ready for the truth. "I don't really know anything about him, hon. All I know is you liked him enough to bring him to the office, which, I'll remind you, you never do. So, the real question is, do you like him?"

Lulu was wrong, she wasn't ready for the truth at all.

Chapter 18

Aiden made it until almost the end of the day Tuesday before he asked. "Rhian, is that a new purse?"

Aiden hoped she would respond something along the lines of this old thing, which his mother often did when he complimented her. He was hoping he had recently developed an eye for noticing things adorned with a swoopy L logo. Sort of like once you decided to buy a new car, it seemed like every car on the street was the make and model you were considering.

"It is," Rhian said, reaching out to pat the item she had placed on top of her desk. It was red and black geometric print that managed to look both bold and understated, in other words it looked very Rhian to him.

"I got a coupon code and couldn't resist," she added.

"It's very you," he said.

"Thanks. I think so too." She tipped her head at him, and he could tell she was deciding whether to ask if he had talked to a certain purse designer. The answer on that was a no.

His apartment no longer smelled like her, and he had discarded the leftovers that had reminded him of her. He had gotten a newsletter about a new exhibit opening next week at the Hirschhorn. He was going to attend and it was going to be excellent, and he wouldn't miss anyone while he was there.

He smiled and hurried back to his office where he finally signed off on the ballroom redesign plans and dug through the rest of his emails. There was always plenty to do.

He finished up at work and metroed home. He tried to remember if he still had a stash of microwave meals or if he had been supposed to grab something on the way home.

He waved at the concierge, in the lobby. Rogan stood, "Uh, sir, you have a visitor." He indicated to his left and there was Lulu. A brilliant burst of hope flooded him before he could stop it, remind himself he had no idea what she was here for. Maybe she had left something behind in his apartment.

"Hi," Lulu said. "I should have called. I definitely should have called. Crap. Sorry, I-"

He put a hand on her shoulder pulling it back quickly before he could think too much about how soft her shoulder was. "Lulu, it's fine. I-" He glanced over at Rogan who stared very intently at his phone. "Come upstairs with me?"

She nodded. They got into the elevator, and he squelched the burgeoning happiness trying to creep up his spine. Lulu just wanted to avoid making a scene, a commotion. She was coming upstairs. It meant nothing else.

He let her into the apartment, and hurried past the entryway deciding the couch was the safest place for them to have a mature discussion. He put his messenger bag down next to the couch.

Lulu hovered next to it.

"Please sit," he said. "I mean, if you want." He stood. "We can stand. I just figured here was more private for whatever."

"I miss you," she said. "I'm sorry I decided it couldn't work because timing and money and whatever else. I miss having fun with you and well, I want to learn all the things we skipped over."

Aiden looked out the picture window, but it still was evening out there. He felt as if the sunshine had reappeared and shined specially on him, warming him.

"Is it too late?" she asked.

Aiden realized he had failed to talk. "Yes, I mean no, it's not too late, yes, I want to try everything with you." He took a step forward afraid his words would trip all over each other again, and he would muddle things.

She stepped forward too and their lips met, and their bodies moved closer together. His hands pulled her close as he tried to tell her with his lips and his tongue how much he wanted to do all of this, how me might already be halfway in love with her.

Much later, as they nibbled on pizza naked in bed, he asked, "So, I'm the exception to the rule then?"

"Which rule?"

He brushed hair out of her eyes, kissing her nose. "The no billionaires rule."

She put her pizza down, licked her fingers slowly, and leaned forward, sliding her arms around his neck, pressing her breasts into his chest. "Oh no," she said softly into his ear, "I'll dump you when you become a billionaire."

He smiled and kissed her. That gave him time to change her mind. He was up to the challenge.

The End

Acknowledgements and Thanks

First, thanks so much for reading this.

I love hearing from readers. Twitter (@TaraTLK) is probably the place I am found most regularly, but I also have a website and a newsletter: http://www.talkapedia.com/p/newsletter.html

If you'd like to leave a review on your review site of choice, I'd appreciate it.

Thanks to all the folks who read this and gave me useful feedback and help. Mistakes as always are mine.

This story, like so many, came about from a combination of ideas. What if dating billionaires was actually boring, because they often relied on flashy dates and then after you were through that initial phase you weren't impressed by what was left? What if someone who had sworn off billionaires accidentally ended up involved with one? What would happen if you flirted too hard or too well on the Amtrak quiet car?

Rafe, who makes an appearance here, appears also in the **Repeated Burn** novella, if you wanted to find out more about what happened when a bakery owner drops his recently dumped sister at his office, and he tries to juggle helping his sister and getting to know said bakery owner.

And once you've made a habit of thanking all the English teachers who supported your writing early and often, it seems foolish to stop. So thanks again. This has been a particularly hard year for teachers, and I send them all my support.

Next in the series:

Clear as Ice

Sienna is no stranger to social media. When she unwittingly starts something claiming there are no Asian Americans in hockey, and then discovers there is one on her hometown team, she knows it's up to her to make amends. And given her new no dating this year rule, she won't have any trouble keeping things professional.

Al is used to people acting like he's the first or only Asian American in hockey. As the Domes' season moves towards the playoffs, he knows how to keep focused just on hockey. Even as Sienna turns out to be more than he expected in so many ways.

Scenes from this were originally posted on my blog for #HockeyFiction. Now the whole story will be available.

About the Author

Tara Kennedy was born and raised in Washington, DC. By day she wrangles data and by night she writes tales of folks smooching and trying to forge their way in this world. Tara also knits, beads, watches TV, and drinks lots and lots of tea. She is trying to break a Twitter habit.

You can find more at www.tarakennedy.com

Also By Tara Kennedy

Bait Girl – A Young Adult Short Story
City Complications Series – Adult Contemporary Romance:
Aloha to You –Novella
Undercover Bridesmaid –Novel
Hot Bartender –Novel
City Entanglements Romance Series: Adult Contemporary Romance:
Repeated Burn – Novella
Bored by the Billionaire – Novella
Clear as Ice – Novella
Not an Ending – a bonus epilogue available to newsletter subscribers
Of Kings and Queens – Novella
Lost in Transit – A bonus short story available to newsletter and Ream
subscribers
Too Busy Romance – Adult Contemporary Romance
Troubled By Love – Novella
Tattoos and Amnesia – A Free Standalone Meet Cute Short
Non-Fiction:
Let's Talk About Fictional Sex
Find info on where to buy them at www.tarakennedy.com/books[1]

---

1. http://www.tarakennedy.com/books

Clear as Ice

Excerpt

C hapter 1
"My ex is so dumb, she thought a face off was when you take off all your make up."

Sienna George sighed and put the phone down. Her business partner Jay had told her to ignore it. Leave it alone. It was wise advice.

She tried to work on her next post for her KeKi leaders group. After a fruitless five minutes that felt like twenty she gave up and grabbed the phone. Her last ex had cleaned out her bank account on his way out the door. This one wanted to build himself up by taking her down. She knew better than to engage. But it was so irritating.

She looked outside her window and had a burst of inspiration. She checked her makeup, everything looked good there. She went outside where some kids had set up a volleyball net. They had even been kind enough to leave the volleyball. She grabbed the ball, and posed in front of the net, taking several selfies.

Posting the photo to Instagram, she captioned it, "What can I say? I've always been more of a volleyball girl, having grown up in Hawaii. Don't see to many folks who look like me playing hockey. #Aloha #Volleyball #WhoNeedsHockey #AAPI

Sienna hit post and felt so much better. It wouldn't stop the ex, but she had such a great batch of followers these days, plus all the folks involved in KeKi.

She went back upstairs and wrote a post for the KeKi leaders about recognizing progress from past mistakes.

JAY: SIENNA.

Sienna smiled. Jay did that a lot. Texted Sienna just her name, leaving Sienna to wonder was this an excited Jay, an exasperated Jay, a Jay who needed coffee, or possibly all of the above. Jay wasn't a morning person either, so usually they saved their communicating for later in the day.

It would be faster to chat. Sienna opened up a video chat, waving when Jay accepted. "Hi, Jay, how are you doing?"

"I thought we agreed you were going to leave it alone." Jay said.

Sienna tipped her head. "We agreed that was a very sensible option, yes." After chatting with some of the folks in the KeKi app, Sienna had fallen asleep watching a movie. She hadn't even remembered to check social media. Or well, she had, but she had seen the text from Jay and not knowing if it was urgent, focused on that first. She hadn't even showered or put on makeup. In fact, she squinted at her face in the corner of the screen, okay, she had remembered to take the makeup off last night. That was at least something.

"Fine," Jay said. "But maybe try not to piss off an entire legion of sports fans for today. Is that a reasonable goal?"

"Yes," Sienna said slowly. Had she already pissed of a legion of sports fans? Sienna was accustomed to making waves on the internet. But she hadn't spent a lot of time on sports. Unless sexy yoga poses counted, but she suspected they did not.

"And when you say yes," Jay said, "so we're on the same page this time, I mean do not piss of any more sports fans today. Sports fans buy things. We like people who buy things."

"Yes," Sienna said.

Jay ended the call and Sienna took a breath and popped open her social media. The most popular response led her to a page of a bearded dude with dark hair and light brown skin. His handle was @UnstoppableTseu.

He had posted a selfie where he pointed at his face. The caption read "Hockey is for everyone, isn't only a saying. There's more work to be done in hockey for sure, but AAPI kids out there, I want you to know there are hockey players like you. #AAPI #AAPIPower #WeAreTheDome

Sienna clicked the #WeAreTheDome hashtag and found a bunch of hockey posts. It appeared to be a hashtag for the local Washington Domes hockey team. And looking at their team roster, Albert Tseu was their goalie. Well shoot. Sienna had pissed off a legion of sports fans, and tried to make a statement about representation without doing the most basic of fact checks. And this Albert Tseu even played for her local team.

Never let it be said that Sienna George couldn't get a lot done early for someone who wasn't naturally a morning person.

Author Note: Clear as Ice *is available at multiple etailers and in print. More info on where to purchase can be found here:* www.tarakennedy.com/books[1]

---

1.   http://www.tarakennedy.com/books

Don't miss out!

Visit the website below and you can sign up to receive emails whenever Tara Kennedy publishes a new book. There's no charge and no obligation.

https://books2read.com/r/B-A-GUVI-MCPTB

BOOKS2READ

Connecting independent readers to independent writers.